To Josh,

Thanks for your interest –

Best wishes,

Kim Russo

SOME THINGS NEVER CHANGE

KURT ALDAG · ILLUSTRATED BY KEN RUSH

MACMILLAN PUBLISHING COMPANY NEW YORK

MAXWELL MACMILLAN CANADA TORONTO
MAXWELL MACMILLAN INTERNATIONAL
NEW YORK OXFORD SINGAPORE SYDNEY

Macmillan Publishing Company is part of the
Maxwell Communication Group of Companies.

Macmillian Publishing Company
866 Third Avenue
New York, NY 10022

Maxwell Macmillan Canada, Inc.
1200 Eglinton Avenue East
Suite 200
Don Mills, Ontario M3C 3N1

FIRST EDITION
Printed in Hong Kong.

10 9 8 7 6 5 4 3 2 1

The text of this book is set in 14 point Aster.
The illustrations are rendered in oil on panel.
Book design by Christy Hale

Library of Congress Cataloging-in-Publication Data
Aldag, Kurt.
Some things never change / Kurt Aldag ; illustrated by Ken Rush. — 1st ed.
p.   cm.
Summary: In a small country town an old man, his granddaughter,
and a gas station attendant discover that some things never change.
ISBN 0-02-700205-5
[1. Time—Fiction. 2. Automobiles—Service stations—Fiction.]
I. Rush, Ken, ill. II. Title.
PZ7.A343So   1992   [E]—dc20   91-9907

For Zoe and Rebecca,
who will always be my little girls

— K.A.

To Christine
and to my children,
George, Andrew, Ann, and Beth

— K.R.

Not many people know about our town. It's not on most maps. It's just a little place along the road. You have to drive forever—up and down the hills, around rock cliffs, past an old farmhouse, a barn, a pasture with cows grazing—until you come to a spot where you can look between the leaves and see the town down in the valley below.

My name is Norman Mack. When you come into town, the first person you see is usually me. I'll be standing out by the gas pumps waiting for a customer, or sitting in a chair reading a newspaper if it's a nice day, or helping my brother Joe and my son Dave with the fuel tank trucks. We own the Mack Brothers Garage.

We get visitors now and then. Almost everybody who comes through stops at our garage for gas and the bathroom and some soda or chips. After all, it's a long way to the next town.

One day an old blue car that was so shiny it looked like
new pulled into the gas station. The driver was a man about
my age with a face I thought I'd seen somewhere before.
There was a passenger in the car, too: a little girl.

The driver looked worried when he got out of his car. His face was puckered up in a frown. I've seen that look on a lot of people's faces when they pull into my station.

"The car's making a funny noise," the man said.

"What kind of noise?" I asked.

"A screeching noise."

"Pop the hood," I said. "Let's take a look."

I had a hunch about the noise and when the hood popped up I reached in to check the fan belt at the front of the engine. I spotted the problem right away. "You need a new fan belt, mister," I said. "This one's stretched and cracked. It's too loose." I pulled on it to show the man how loose it was. "It will take a couple of minutes to change."

The man was staring down the road, lost in thought. There was something about his gaze that made me think I really *had* seen him somewhere before.

"You live around here?" I asked, thinking maybe that's why he looked so familiar.

"Not anymore," he answered. "My family moved away years ago. We used to live up the road a ways, a couple of towns north of here. I haven't been back in a long time." The man glanced at the sign over our garage door, and then looked me in the eye and said, "I wanted to take a drive up this way to see if things had changed."

"This town used to be a lot bigger until the mill closed down," I said. "That's when a lot of people moved away. Even my brother Joe moved away," I told him. "But he came back because he missed the old place."

Then I looked at the car and thought it was a lot like my father's old blue sedan—the first new car we ever owned. It was a beauty. We drove it for a long, long time. Joe and I learned to fix engines by working on it. That's how we got started in business. Finally, it got to be so much trouble to fix that my father had to sell it. I remember that day. An old farmer and his son came to pick it up. I was sorry to see it go down the road that last time.

"You might want to go over to the old mill," I said, trying to think of things the two of them could do while I looked around for a fan belt. "When you go inside, the wind whistling through the eaves and rafters sounds like people talking." I leaned over to look in the car window at the little girl, and asked, "You want to go over there and explore?" But I could see by the look in her eyes that the mill sounded pretty scary to her.

"I'm afraid she's—she's—" the man's mustache twitched. "She's afraid."

"Afraid?" I asked, sticking my head in the window.

She hid her face in her hands.

"There's nothing to be afraid of around here," I said. "The old mill's nothing but a big birdhouse now. You'll find some fine feathers in there. You could make a headdress from the feathers."

The little girl's eyes opened wide and she asked, "Can we, Gramps?" She slid across the car seat and opened the door. "Oh, please, Gramps. Let's go hunting for beautiful bird feathers."

"That's a wonderful idea," he said, taking her hand in his.

So off they went while I began looking for a fan belt. The trouble was, I didn't know if I had one that would fit. The car was an antique, even though it looked like new. And then I remembered: I'd kept some parts for that old blue four-door.

Sure enough, there was an old fan belt hanging on the wall in the garage. It had been there for as long as I could remember. It was a little dusty, but it would work like new, I figured.

I took it out to the car. It looked like it would fit perfectly so I began loosening the fan with a wrench. I was just about to slip the new belt into place when I heard Blue barking. Blue's my hound dog. It sounded like he was over by the old mill. Uh-oh, I thought. He'll scare the little girl.

I was beginning to worry about them when the girl and her grandfather appeared in the doorway. She had a fistful of feathers—some long, some short, some black, some white.

Blue followed them in and sat down right next to her.

"I see you met Blue," I said.

"He gave us a little scare there for a second," said the girl's grandfather.

"He's all bark and no bite," I said.

"Why do you call him Blue?" the little girl asked, scratching the dog's ear as if they were old buddies.

"Because when he's hunting, I can hear him in the woods. And it sounds like he's saying *b-l-u-u-u-u-e* when he's got the scent of a rabbit."

Joe walked in with Dave and said, "Say Norman, that sure does look like the car Dad had, doesn't it? I wonder what happened to that old jalopy."

Just as he said that, it dawned on me.

"You're not going to believe this, Joe," I said. "But I think that car out there used to be our old clunker."

"What?" said Joe. "That just can't be."

"Yes," said the man. "That's it. When I saw the sign, I thought I knew the name from somewhere. I remember now. Your father—Henry Mack, right?"

"That's right," said Joe. "Henry Mack."

"He sold my father this car," said the man. "And my father fixed it up like new and gave it to me."

"I thought you looked familiar," I said, remembering the day the farmer and his son came to the garage many, many years ago.

We all had a good chuckle.

When it was time for them to get back on the road I walked out to the car with them.

"Can't we get some more feathers, Gramps?" the little girl asked.

"Oh, no, honey," he answered. "It's getting late and it's a long way to the next town. Say good-bye to Blue."

"You come back and visit again some day," I said. "I'll show you where you might find an owl feather."

"Good-bye, Blue," she said, giving him a big hug. "I'll come back to hunt with you again sometime." The little girl climbed in the front seat next to her grandfather and sat where I used to sit when my father drove the car. Her grandfather put the key in the ignition and started the engine. The old blue car sounded like new again.

As they drove off, I waved and they waved back. But this time, watching the old blue car head down the road, I wasn't sorry to see it go.

I figure the little girl and the old blue car will come back. When she's all grown-up, she'll drive it to the Mack Brothers Garage to get some gas from my son, Dave.

Seeing that old blue car again all shiny like new, I realized that cars and people come and go, but some things never change.